Pet-napping Mystery

Adapted by Dandi Daley Mackall
Illustrated by Mike Young Productions

Based on *The Puzzle Club Pet-napping Mystery* original story
by Mark Young for Lutheran Hour Ministries

Lutheran Hour
Ministries

Published by Concordia Publishing House, 3558 S. Jefferson Avenue, St. Louis, MO 63118-3968
Manufactured in the United States of America

2   3   4   5   6   7   8   9   10   08   07   06   05   04   03   02   01   00

Korina could not believe it! Her science teacher *had* to know that she was the best scientist in New Bristol Junior High. So why give her loudmouth, bubble-gum-chewing Riley Gadwalder for a lab partner?

Now Riley wouldn't leave her alone. "I've got tons of great ideas at home for our science project, Korina," he announced.

"Then go home and get them, Riley!" Korina snapped. She pointed to the gum wrappers that fell at his feet like dandruff. "And pick up your litter!" She turned on her heels and stomped away.

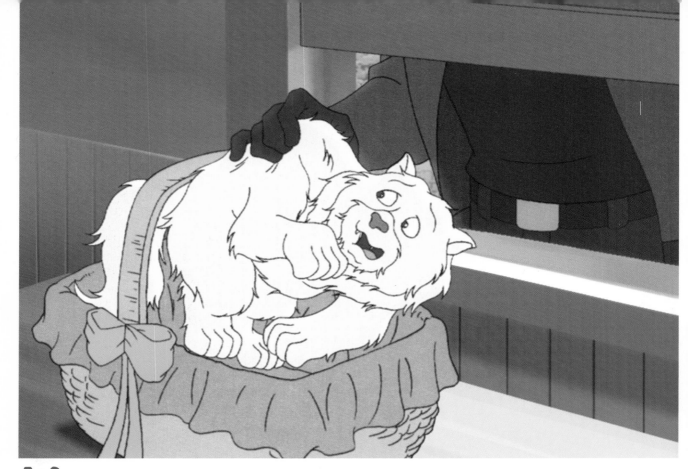

Meanwhile, on the other side of town, unsuspecting pets lie sleeping in their beds, never dreaming what shadowy, sinister evil lurks just outside the window.

Napping pets, beware of pet-nappers!

As foul play continues to strike the city of New Bristol, not even a toucan is safe! Will nobody come to the rescue of innocent furry or feathered friends? Is there no one to stop this persistent, pet-thieving pet-napper?

Korina left Riley talking to himself and headed straight for Puzzle Club headquarters, which was located in the secret attic of Tobias' Puzzleworks Shop. Her old friend Tobias was singing to himself when Korina flung open the door.

"Good afternoon, Korina," Tobias called cheerfully.

Korina stomped past him without so much as a glance. "What's so good about it?" she mumbled.

Korina punched in the secret code to deactivate the Puzzle Club's alarm system. Then she stormed into headquarters and slammed the door behind her. The puppy Alex was trying to find a home for scampered to greet her.

"Call off Watson, Alex!" she yelled. "One lost cause is enough for today. Guess who I got stuck with as lab partner—that pest, Riley Gadwalder!"

Sherlock, the Puzzle Club's parakeet mascot, looked as shocked at her outburst as Alex. Watson dove into Alex's arms.

"Korina," Alex said, inching toward the door, "do you remember what Tobias told me about the 'dragon lady' who takes tickets at the movies? Tobias said God helped him see that she's not really mean—just shy."

"Well, Riley Gadwalder is *not* shy!" Korina exclaimed.

Alex left for the pet shop to buy dog food and to try to find a home for Watson. Korina paced around headquarters. "Nobody appreciates my scientific superiority," Korina mumbled. "Not Mr. I-Know-Everything Riley Gadwalder. Not even Alex! After all, Alex couldn't even handle that puppy if it weren't for *my* invention!" *She* was the one who had sewn a microchip into Watson's collar to direct him right or left or even to stay.

Christopher, the Puzzle Club's fearless leader, stopped developing photos. "Don't be so quick to judge Riley, Korina."

"Easy for you to say!" she snapped. "You're not stuck with him."

An hour later, Korina and Christopher were discussing their new cases when Korina heard a loud *POP!* She turned to see Riley swinging on a rope outside the window. He swung inside, chomping his gum as usual.

"Hey, partner," Riley called. "I decided our science project will be neutrino particle detection."

Korina fumed. "Nuclear physicists can't even do that," she said.

Before Riley could reply, the phone rang. Christopher answered it. "A missing cat?" he said. "That's odd."

Korina was about to tell Christopher to ask if the cat simply might be having kittens when Alex and Sherlock burst into headquarters.

"Something awful happened at the pet shop!" Alex cried. "Watson's vanished!"

Hasn't the great Puzzle Club heard about all the pet-nappings in New Bristol?" Riley asked. He dug a peanut out of his pocket and gave it to Sherlock.

Christopher spoke into the phone. "Mr. Gregali, we'll be right over to look for your cat."

Instead of leaving like he *should* have, Riley scratched Sherlock's head. "I wish I had a pet of my own," he said. "I have a theory about these pet-nappings—"

We don't need your theories!" Korina shouted, pushing Riley out the door.

"You didn't have to be mean," Alex said when Riley had gone. Christopher nodded in agreement.

Korina sizzled inside. "Why don't you two mind your own business? Riley Gadwalder is an impossible pest, and that's all there is to it."

As Tobias drove The Puzzle Club to Mr. Gregali's house, Korina couldn't concentrate on the case. She kept thinking about what a pest Riley was.

When they arrived at the home of Pete Gregali, Alex and Sherlock examined the cat's basket. Christopher took pictures, and Korina checked for fingerprints.

"You're sure your cat didn't just run away?" Tobias asked.

Mr. Gregali frowned. "Jezebel was stolen. You're wasting my time, Tobias. And you kids better not break anything! I'm calling Sheriff Grimaldi to get some *real* help."

Mr. Gregali thundered off to call the sheriff.

Korina joined Tobias. "He's almost as obnoxious as Riley," she said. "How can you be nice to someone like that?"

Tobias grinned. "Maybe it's because I don't see him the way others do. He's just worried about Jezebel. When I look at Mr. Gregali, I remember that none of us is perfect and that God loves and accepts all of us because of Jesus. That helps me see others in a different way."

Korina stared at Tobias. "I just don't see it the way you do," she said.

"Well, it's not easy," he admitted, smiling as he removed his glasses. "Sometimes I put these on to remind me to see others as God sees them."

He held his glasses out to Korina. "Want to try?"

Korina waved away Tobias' glasses. "No thanks," she said. Tobias just didn't understand.

After receiving an urgent call from a toucan owner, The Puzzle Club raced to investigate the latest pet-napping. Korina let the others conduct the interview while she searched for clues.

"Please find Mr. Timothy," she heard the bird's owner plead.

"Don't worry, ma'am," Christopher answered. "If there are clues to your toucan's disappearance, The Puzzle Club will find them."

Through her trusty magnifying glass, Korina spotted something in the grass. She picked it up and ran to show the others.

"Case solved!" Korina exclaimed, showing Alex, Christopher, and Tobias the clue she had discovered. "A gum wrapper. And who chews this brand of bubble gum and drops wrappers everywhere?"

"Almost every kid in town?" Alex offered.

"No!" Korina shouted. "Riley Gadwalder. *He's* our pet-napper!"

Tobias shook his head. "That's not enough evidence to prove anything, Korina," he said.

"Sure it is," she insisted. "He said he wanted a pet."

"But why would Riley steal a toucan *and* a cat?" Christopher asked.

"Yeah," Alex agreed. "Don't jump to conclusions, Korina."

That did it. "Well, if you won't believe me," she announced, "I'll find some-one who will!"

Korina ran to Sheriff Grimaldi's office and told him Riley was the pet-napper. The sheriff called Riley and asked him to come to the police station. When he arrived, Sheriff Grimaldi showed Riley the evidence—the gum wrapper from the scene of the crime.

"Korina has helped solve a lot of mysteries around town," said Sheriff Grimaldi. "Riley, I'm going to ask that you stay home with your mother for a while."

Korina couldn't help smiling to herself—Riley Gadwalder was under house arrest.

"But I'm not a thief, Sheriff," Riley protested. "I wish you'd believe me."

"Son," said the sheriff, "it's just for a few days."

Riley shuffled out the door. "I haven't done anything wrong," he mumbled. "You'll see."

The sheriff was just glad to have the kids out of harm's way.

Korina returned to headquarters. She was thumbing through her science book when in walked Christopher and Alex.

"You shouldn't have gone to the sheriff without us, Korina," Christopher scolded. "What if you're wrong about Riley?"

"We're a team," Alex said. "And we can't accuse somebody without evidence."

Korina slammed her book shut. "You're just jealous that I solved the mystery. Riley is *definitely* the pet-napper."

Meanwhile, figuring nobody will believe him until the real pet-napper is unmasked, Riley sneaks out of his house to search for clues. At the home of the missing toucan, Riley picks up a feather that puts him hot on the pet-napper's trail.

At Puzzle Club headquarters, you could cut the tension with a knife. Sherlock played with Korina's electronic dog leash invention, turning the knob left and right. Alex paced the floor muttering, "Poor Watson."

"Alex," Korina reassured him, "it's only a matter of time before Riley talks. Staying home alone has to be getting to him."

Riley is almost always home alone," Christopher said. "His parents are divorced and his mom has two jobs."

Korina thought about how awful that would be. "I didn't know that," she said. She'd never thought much about Riley, except about how annoying he was. When she did think about it, she had to admit that even *she* could be annoying sometimes. What if she'd been wrong about Riley all along?

Tobias said God loved and accepted everybody because of Jesus. Korina thought about how much it meant to her to have a friend like Jesus, someone who forgave her and loved her even when she was annoying.

Sherlock knocked over Korina's electro-leash invention, and Korina picked it up.

"Wait a minute!" she shouted. "If I switch a couple of wires and use this condenser, I can turn Watson's collar into an Electro-Leash Dog *Finder*. And once we find Watson, we'll find the pet-napper!"

Korina was just about to test the Dog Finder when a loud, scratchy sound came from her desk. "*Puzzle Club?*" the sheriff's raspy voice came over the CB radio. "*This is Sheriff Grimaldi. Riley Gadwalder is missing!*"

Korina, Christopher, Alex, and Sherlock followed the beeping Electro-Leash. It took them down side streets, over fences, and all the way to an abandoned warehouse.

Riley ran away because he's guilty, Korina thought. *Good.* She didn't want to think of him as the kid who always got left by himself. It was easier to keep the picture in her head of Riley the Obnoxious Lab Partner or Riley the Pet-napper.

As The Puzzle Club entered the smelly warehouse, they saw cages of whimpering, stolen pets. Tied to a chair was Riley Gadwalder.

"I'm not the pet-napper," Riley said weakly as they untied him. "I was following a trail of bird feathers when he nabbed *me*! The guy is hiding out here until he can sell the animals."

Korina felt terrible. She heard Tobias' voice in her head: *I put on these glasses to remind me to see others as God sees them.* "Riley," she said, "I'm sorry for all the mean things I said. I just didn't see."

Riley smiled at Korina. "We've got to get out of here before—"

"Don't move, you kids!" Blocking the doorway stood a tall, angry-looking man. "You're gonna wish you never found me!" he yelled.

Something crashed to the floor behind the pet-napper. The snarling Watson charged from his broken cage to bite the villain's ankle!

*Y*eow!" cried the pet-napper, trying to shake off Watson.

"Way to go, Watson!" Alex cheered.

But The Puzzle Club wasn't out of danger. As the pet-napper made his escape, he bumped into a table, knocking over his coffeepot and red-hot burner. Flames burst from a pile of old newspapers where the burner landed. The fire spread through the old, wooden warehouse.

As the warehouse filled with smoke, the sound of frightened dogs, cats, and other beasts hammered Korina's ears.

"The animals!" cried Riley.

With arms full of cages and pets, The Puzzle Club plus Riley raced out of the burning warehouse.

Outside, Korina spied the pet-napper running across the street. "He's getting away!" she cried as a police car zoomed on the scene.

Tobias and Sheriff Grimaldi jumped out and made the capture.

Safe back at headquarters, The Puzzle Club presented Riley with his very own pet—Watson.

"You can keep each other company," Korina said as Watson licked Riley's face.

"Thanks, partner!" Riley exclaimed. "And don't worry about that science project. I already have a theory."

Not this again, Korina thought. But this time she reached over and borrowed Tobias' glasses. "Let's discuss it … partner."

Korina smiled at Riley. She had a feeling she'd be borrowing Tobias' glasses quite a bit from now on.